THE TOO-SCARY STORY

Bethanie Deeney Murguia

SCHOLASTIC INC.

For Phil, the storyteller

ISBN 978-1-338-23074-1

Arthur A. Levine Books hardcover edition published by Arthur A. Levine Books, an imprint of Scholastic Inc., July 2017

12 11 10 9 8 7 6 5 4 3 2 1   17 18 19 20 21 22

Printed in the U.S.A.   40

First Scholastic paperback printing, September 2017

The art was created with pencil, watercolor, gouache, and hand-painted tissue collage.
The title was hand-lettered by Bethanie Deeney Murguia.
The text was set in Baskerville Regular and Two Fingers Bodoni.
Art direction by Marijka Kostiw
Book design by Bethanie Deeney Murguia and Marijka Kostiw

One dark night,
in a house on a hill . . .

Papa asks, "How about a bedtime story?"

"Yes!" exclaims Walter.

"Make it a scary story," says Grace.
"I've got my wand."

"All right," says Papa.

One night, two brave explorers
and their dog were walking home
through the forest. It was very, very . . .

dark.

"Yes! The spookiest, creepiest kind of dark!" says Grace.

"Too scary!" says Walter.

Well, as they ran out of the woods,
hundreds of tiny, twinkling lights appeared.

"Fireflies!" Walter cheers.

"Papa, fireflies are *not* scary," says Grace. "I want to see bears!"

"Just a minute," says Papa.

Beyond the fireflies,
deep in the bushes, crept all kinds of . . .

creatures.

"I can hear them all *breathing*," whispers Grace.

"Too scary!" says Walter.

Don't worry.
Those creatures were just
settling into bed for the night.

"Sleep tight," Walter whispers.

"I hope that's not the end of the story,"
mutters Grace.

"Oh, there's more," says Papa.

Not everyone was ready for bed.
Faintly at first, and then louder,
the children heard . . .

footsteps.

"Don't worry, Walter. I have my wand," says Grace.

Their dog growled a long, low growl.
Just behind them on the path was a . . .

shadow.

"Does your wand work on shadows?" whispers Walter.

"I'm not sure," Grace whispers back.

The children dashed home,
up the stairs, and into their room,
slamming the door behind them.

"Papa, nothing in the closet, please," begs Grace.

"Or under the bed," whispers Walter.

". . . Papa, are you there?"

Creeeeeak.

The bedroom door began to open.

"Be gone, shadow monster!"

Grace shouts.

"It worked! I turned that evil shadow into Papa!" Grace says.

"I wasn't scared at all," adds Walter.

"Um . . . Papa? Can we sleep with the light on?" asks Grace.

"I have a better idea," says Papa.

"Good night, my brave explorers."

Bethanie Deeney Murguia

is the author and illustrator of *Princess! Fairy! Ballerina!*, *Zoe Gets Ready*, *Zoe's Room (No Sisters Allowed)*, and *Zoe's Jungle*, among several other beloved picture books. She loves to hear scary stories, as long as the light is on and the closet door is closed. Please visit her website at www.aquapup.com or find her on Twitter at @aquapup.

Things Bethanie Would Not Like to Encounter in The Dark Woods:

- Dinosaurs, of any kind
- A troupe of clowns
- Pale green pants with nobody inside them (thanks, Dr. Seuss)